Dump Truck Dash

Peter Bently

Illustrated by Martha Lightfoot

NEW
BURLINGTON
BOOKS

Beaver climbs into Dump Truck's cab
and starts the **powerful** engine.

A new town hall is being built because
the old one was **damaged** in a fire.

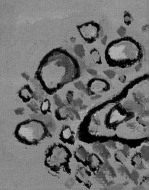

Dump Truck is helping **clear** the building site.

Dump Truck and Beaver are going to **recycle** as much of the old material as possible.

They take a load of **scrap metal**
to the bicycle factory.

Then they take a load of **soil** to the new park.

Back on the building site, Bulldozer clears away the old building into big piles.

CRUNCH!

Digger **picks UP** rubble in its scoop . . .

CRASH!

. . . and **drops** the rubble into Dump Truck's strong tipper.

They **fill** in the new town hall's foundations.
Beaver pulls the lever, and Dump Truck's tipper
slowly tilts up and the rubble pours out.

WHIRR!

"Well done,"
says Beaver.
"Let's get another load."

It starts to rain. Beaver turns on Dump Truck's **windshield wipers** so he can see through the windshield.

Dump Truck is **big and tough** and can work in any weather. This means that Beaver can move a lot of rubble very quickly.

Now the rain is **pouring** down.
A police car arrives.

WOO-WOO-WOO!

"The river is about to burst its banks,"
says the Police Officer. "The flood will head this way!
Everyone must **leave** the building site."

From high up in Dump Truck's cab, Beaver can see where the river is close to **overflowing**.

"I have an idea!" he says.

Digger **helps** load Dump Truck with the rest of the rubble.

When the tipper is **full**, Beaver and Dump Truck set off.

"That's the **wrong** way!" cries the Police Officer.
"You're heading for the river!"

"**Don't worry,**" says Beaver.
"We know what we're doing!"

Beaver and Dump Truck **hurry**
toward the river.

SPLASH!

The heavy rain has made deep puddles, but Dump Truck's **huge wheels** keep the engine out of the water.

SPLOSH!

Dump Truck's **big tires** stop them from skidding in the mud.

Beaver reaches the riverbank.
He sees where the water
is starting to **overflow**.

Beaver **carefully**
backs up and pulls the lever.

Dump Truck **tips** the rubble into place.

Beaver and Dump Truck watch as the rubble **stops** the river from overflowing. "We did it!" cries Beaver.

Back at the building site, everyone is pleased.

"Well done, Beaver!" they cry.

"Thanks," says Beaver, "but Dump Truck is the real hero. Well done, Dump Truck!"

Let's look at
Dump Truck

Exhaust
pipe

Tipper

Lever

Hydraulic
arm

Big tires

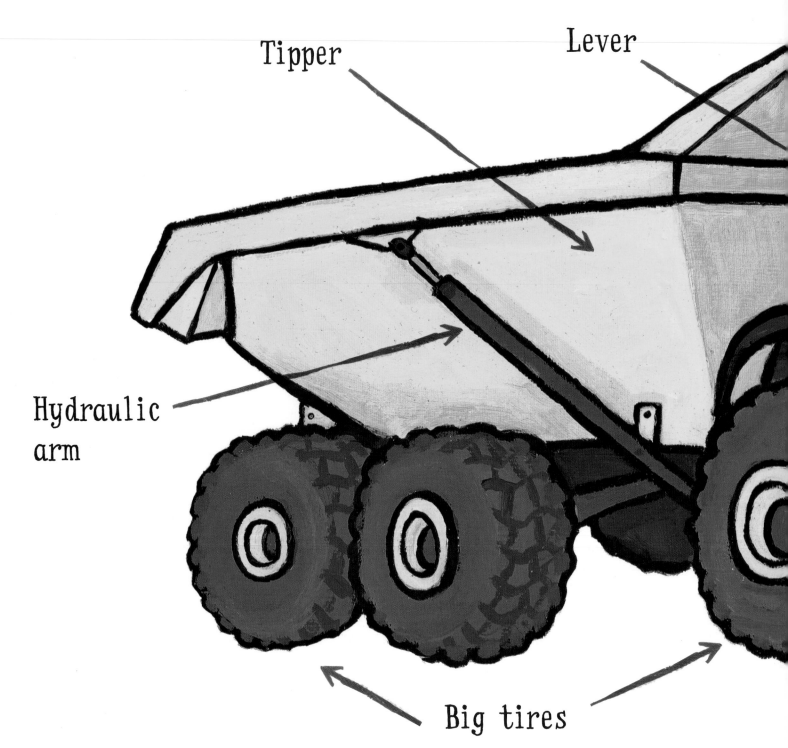

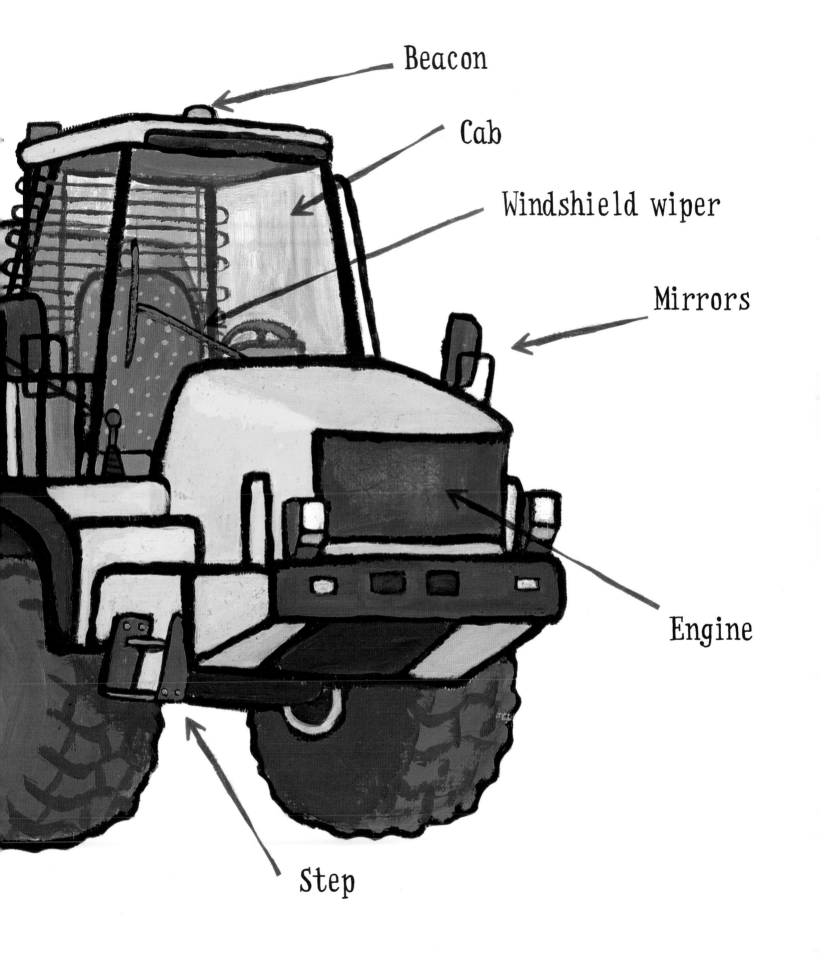

Beacon

Cab

Windshield wiper

Mirrors

Engine

Step

Other Building Machines

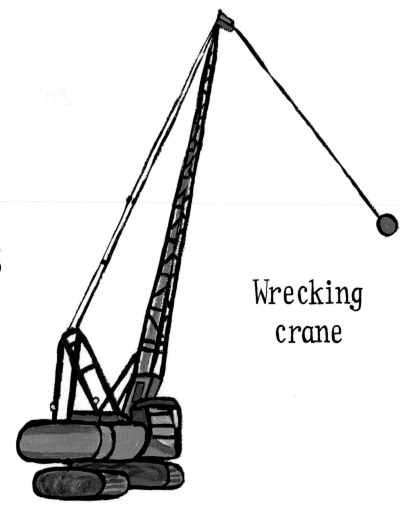

Wrecking crane

Cement-mixer truck

Bulldozer

Digger

For my mum and dad, with love. M.L.

For Eli. P.B.

A NEW BURLINGTON BOOK
The Old Brewery
6 Blundell Street
London N7 9BH

Designer: Plum5 Limited
Project Editor: Lucy Cuthew
Editorial Assistant: Tasha Percy

First published in the United States in 2013 by
QEB Publishing, Inc.
3 Wrigley, Suite A
Irvine, CA 92618

www.qed-publishing.co.uk

A CIP record for this book is available from the Library of Congress.

ISBN: 978 1 78171 394 5

Printed in China